GIANT DAYS™

EARLY REGISTRATION

BOOM! BOX™

For information regarding the CPSIA on this printed material, call: (203) 595-3636 and provide reference #RICH – 812283.

BOOM! Studios, 5670 Wilshire Boulevard, Suite 400, Los Angeles, CA 90036-5679. Printed in USA. First Printing.

ISBN: 978-1-68415-265-0, eISBN: 978-1-64144-276-3

LAAAAA!
SHELLAC
INGWALKER

GIANT DAYS™

EARLY REGISTRATION

WRITTEN + ILLUSTRATED BY
JOHN ALLISON

COVER BY
JOHN ALLISON

DESIGNER
JILLIAN CRAB

ASSISTANT EDITOR
SOPHIE PHILIPS-ROBERTS

EDITOR
SHANNON WATTERS

CHAPTER ONE

I remember when I first came away to university, Esther.
It feels like yesterday.
We packed up Grandpop's car with all my things, my whole life...
...and drove the lot to Exeter.
Mother and father went and left me in that little room.
Peter don't! You'll upset her.
Go on, Daddy.
I propped open my door, lit a joss stick, and played a Leonard Cohen record.
You know, to show I was *interesting*. Then I went to sleep.
Daughter, do not underestimate the icebreaking potential of a small fire.

Bye bye daddy.
Little one, we are so proud of you.
You'll be having the time of your life in no time.
Call us if you need anything, sweetheart.
CLICK
SNIF
BONK
SQUEAK
Um yes... if it's not..
Do you need a hand?
SQUEAK
BONK
...too much trouble...
D.A.M
I got half-way up but a load of girls came down so I had to go to the bottom again.
Oh, delightful.
I didn't think it was *delightful*. I thought it was a bit *rude*.
BONK
Riiiiight.

Flipping hell, what's in this thing? Nazi gold?
No! All my things! For university!
BONK
I had to bring it down on the train.
Separate items... are sometimes easier to carry
One big trunk is easier than lots of bags.
SHUF
Couldn't someone give you a ride down?
RUB RUB
No, I-
Excuse me
Some of us are trying to sleep.
Were you *smoking* in your sleep?
Erk. Well, I'm Daisy.
Esther! Esther de Groot!
Hi, hi, Susan Ptolemy
SHAKE
13
And I've not slept
IN A WEEK

Should we have asked Susan Ptolemy if she wanted to come to dinner with us?
Did you want to wake S. Ptolemy up again? Because I didn't!
BRR!
Let the beast sleep.
I don't think *this* would have improved her mood
We might have to go and find something later. We don't want to starve and die.
GORK
Shall we go to the hall bar later?
It's SUB-SI-DISED!
I've... I've never had an alcohol drink.
Ha ha ha! You're a funny one, Daisy.
Let's unpack for a bit, come and give me a knock at eight.
You're the most confident person I've ever met!
I didn't mean to say that out loud.
SLAM

It's primitive! The bed mattress is like 5cm thick.
My room is en-suite.
I think we have to wash in the communal bowl
Is the water communal or just the bowl
KNOCK KNOCK
I knew Daisy was an *early* not a *late*.
ALARM1
19:39
BIMPO
DAB
Hi *Esther*, we're from down the corridor,
We're here to take you for a drink.
Oh er... hello
Um ok, we just need to get Daisy.
12
She means "Lollipop".
Oh, she's gone down to the bar already.
Come on, first night, let's go MENTAL.
12
That sounds...
...great.

Esther? Esther! Hello!
Are you asleep?
12
TAP TAP TAP TAP TAP TAP TAP TAP TAP TAP
I WAS asleep, Daisy. For eight *amazing* minutes.
Oh sorry Susan!
It's all right. Like most people, you were born noisy.
The populars came and got Esther.
POPULARS?
Yeah, hard faced witches with expensive paid-for educations
I think they mistook your friend for a kindred spirit.
Is she one?
Nah, she's your classic ugly duckling.
Born on the outside looking in, then "goes swan" late on.
I... I like what you've done with the place.
No you don't.
I'm pretty sure this one's a *goose*.

Anyway he wouldn't pay to insure my car at uni so I like... tell him...
...flip you, I'm asking mummy instead.
CATTERICK HALL OF RESIDENCE BAR
It was only like £3000. Guh.
I know oh god I *know*, mine only gives me £300 a month for clothes.
Oh em gee you poor *peasant*.
So anyway *Esther*, tell us about you. Have you got a boyfriend?
God you know she does, like a total stud boy.
Alll tattoos and everything pierced, right?
SPILL.
SAMBUCAS GUYS, WOO!
SLOSH
DOOK
DOOK
DOOK
DOOK
I bet he's got a SERIOUS drug habit, right?
I'm thinking of getting one of those.

...so where are you from, Susan?
Daisy Wooton had a body like a bicycle frame and hair like wild heather.
Eyes like Bambi ten seconds before momma got the bullet.
MENU
CURRY GOAT
AFRICAN CARIBBEAN
JERK CHICKEN
Northampton. They say when you're tired of Northampton, you're tired of life.
But I had to get out for a while. Let the heat die down.
Oxfam
PAKISTAN FLOOD APPEAL
Yes, it has been a warm summer. I'm from-
Let me guess.
It's a hamlet, four or five houses where two B roads cross in the middle of nowhere.
Once a day, the neighbour-hood crow flies over and gives you something to look at.
Don't be silly!
There's no such thing as a "neighbour-hood crow".

Esther it was really funny how you kept pretending you had to leave.
You're HILARIOUS, we LOVE you.
BFF!
SWIPE
Flip I'm hungry, I have the munchies so bad.
Look at all this FOOD!
It's LOLLIPOP'S! She put her NAME on it! Aww!
We should do something to thank her.
NAM NAM
Get her a paper bag for her head.
Hey, don't eat that!
Oo, Esther's a MORALIST, mm!
I hope your morals taste as good as these scones, YUM
Ha!
OK, let's all meet for breakfast tomorrow.
BFF!
BFF!
BFF!
I don't feel... all that good
I will destroy EACH AND EVERY ONE OF YOU.

RAP RAP RAP
Oh er I was just doing my yoga.
Daisy! I thought maybe we wouldn't have breakfast in the dining hall....
I brought you breakfast in bed.
Did you see the trail of devastation out there?
Oh sorry Susan, did I wake you up?
No, some-one was playing Enya at 6.45. ENYA.
TO DAISY, ALL MY LOVE
enya
Those vile girls down the hall made the mess. Ugh.
I saw one of them managed to puke in a perfect parabolic arc.
They kidnapped me and talked for HOURS without actually saying anything.
I hope you tried to kill them with your mind.
scff
SHOES ON THE BED!

Archeology Daisy? Really?
I've always been interested in it!
Well I hope the other archeologists are er... *borderline normal.*
This is the Dick Bruna Building, this is me!
See you later!
Bye Esther!
Hello, are you here for English Literature?
Yes I am.
I'm Ed Gemmell.
Esther.
You can sit down, but you can't ask me what I did for my A-Levels.
I've answered that question 200 times this week.
It's the ice breaker du jour.
What if our answers are lies?
Yes, ok. I did Jazz Dance, Tunnel Studies and Poisons.
I did Fighting, Further Fighting and History (Of Fights)
It's left me quite tired.

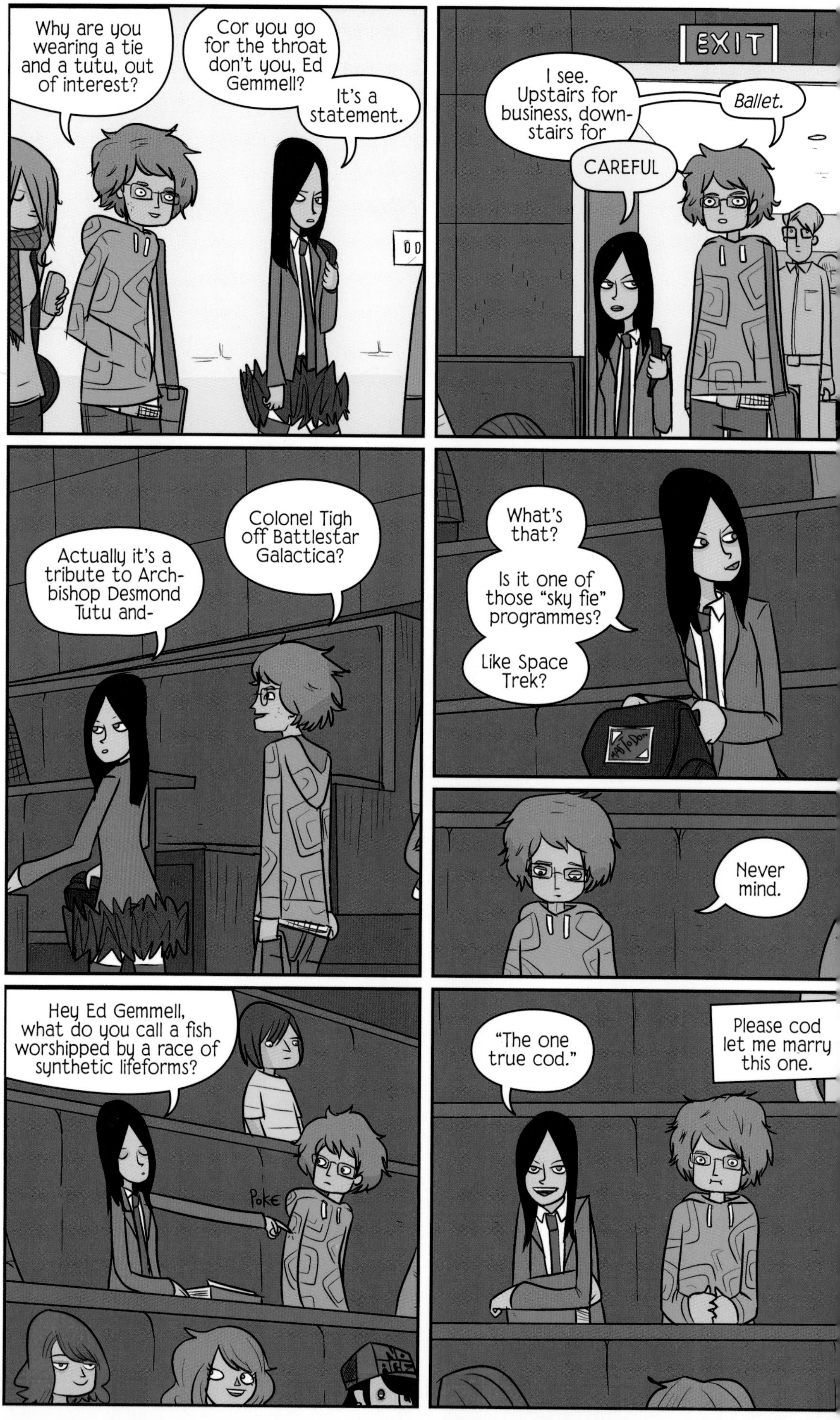

Why are you wearing a tie and a tutu, out of interest?
Cor you go for the throat don't you, Ed Gemmell?
It's a statement.
EXIT
I see. Upstairs for business, down-stairs for
Ballet.
CAREFUL
Actually it's a tribute to Arch-bishop Desmond Tutu and-
Colonel Tigh off Battlestar Galactica?
What's that?
Is it one of those "sky fie" programmes?
Like Space Trek?
Never mind.
Hey Ed Gemmell, what do you call a fish worshipped by a race of synthetic lifeforms?
POKE
"The one true cod."
Please cod let me marry this one.

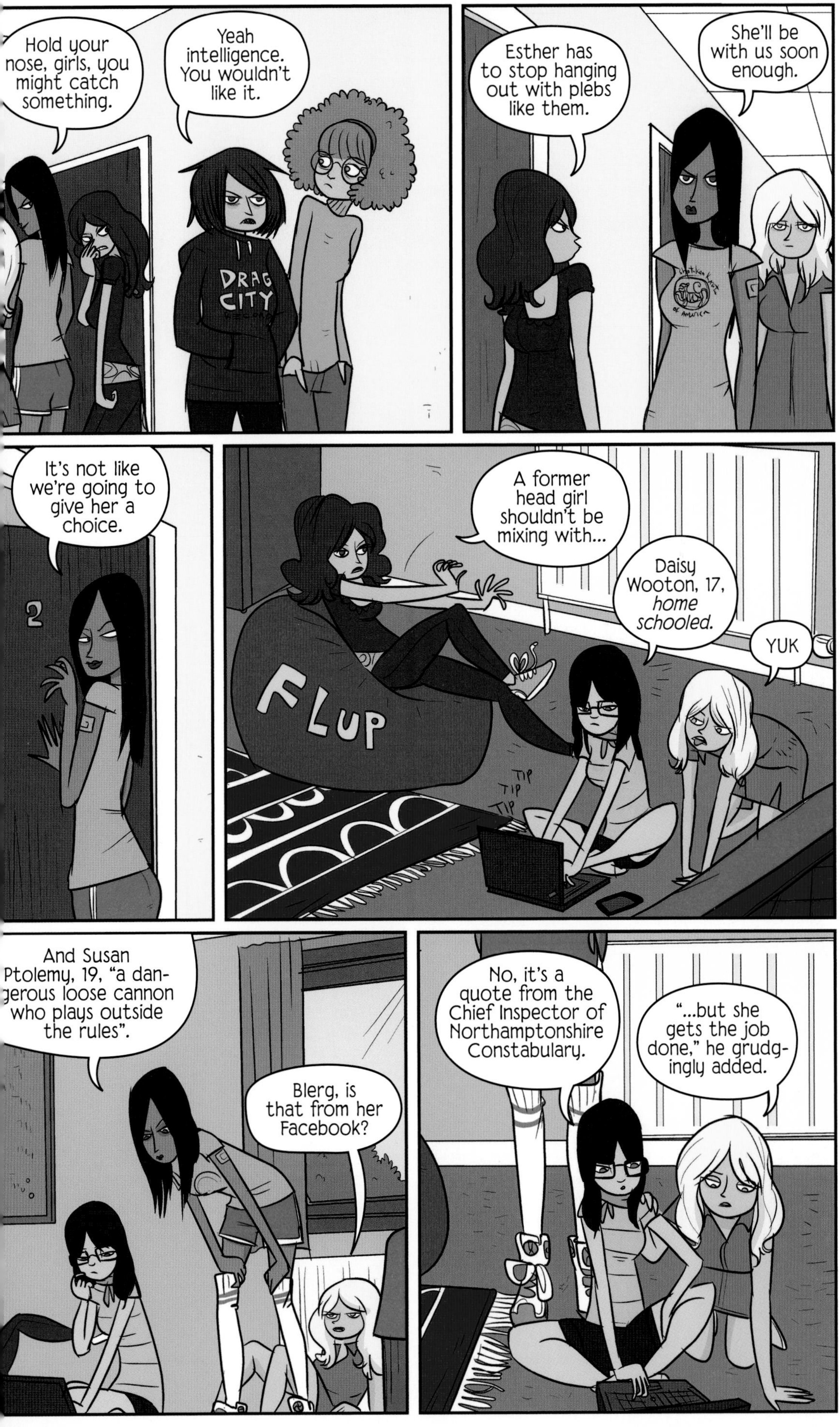

Hold your nose, girls, you might catch something.
Yeah intelligence. You wouldn't like it.
Esther has to stop hanging out with plebs like them.
She'll be with us soon enough.
It's not like we're going to give her a choice.
A former head girl shouldn't be mixing with...
Daisy Wooton, 17, *home schooled.*
YUK
TIP TIP TIP
FLUP
And Susan Ptolemy, 19, "a dangerous loose cannon who plays outside the rules".
Blerg, is that from her Facebook?
No, it's a quote from the Chief Inspector of Northamptonshire Constabulary.
"...but she gets the job done," he grudgingly added.

Well look at you two!
Esther! Hay Esther!
Are you coming with us to the dance? Dancing!
You like the sort of person who likes Dancing, Esther.
I like to move to... certain sounds.
Don't try to make me dance. I'm going to be STANDING.
Let me quickly get out of my swimming pool clothes!
FIF
BLUST
Z
P
1 hour 31 minutes! A record!
PIP
01:31
Oh there you are, I was just coming to get you.
The povs have arranged a disco so we can laugh at them all in one place.
I think the phone number you gave me is wrong.
They're not usually 40 digits long.
12

IT'S SO LOUD!
WHERE'S ESTHER? IT'S BEEN AGES!
Girls like Esther take a lot of launching
like a new car
OH I SEE HER!!!
HEELLP
OH NO... SHE'S GESTURE ILLITERATE
Clear off, Lollipop
Hey!
What's your problem, Witch Hazel?
I just wanted to tell you what time it is.
IT'S GO TIME

BIFF
You shouldn't have done that, BABA YAGA.
Ow yeah you're probably right.
Oh god, Susan's *mental for fights.*
You see, to be head girl of a prestigious English school...
...you have to have mastered a *fighting style.*
ANNA TREVELLIAN
TEAM GB CAPTAIN,
TAEKWONDO
But I don't think we'll have to use any of them to end YOU.
WHOA THERE
KRACK
MIN OTOMO
DRUNKEN MASTER
Sit down, gothy.
It's for your own good.
Tangentially speaking.
Shove
NITA KAPOOR
NO STYLE

Daisy! Pull yourself together! Help me get them off Susan!
BIF
BAF
BIF
KICK
Esther are you all right?
Oh just CAPITAL, Ed Gemmell.
Take my key and get the bag from under my bed-
-AND DON'T DITHER!
HUF
PUF
HUF
PUF
RATTLE
RATTLE
THE SECRET WORLD OF WOMEN!
SMELLS SO NICE
SUCH A MESS

Oh Christ, everything is so SCANTY
Can't concentrate
Bag, Ed! UNDER BED
FIGHT THIS
TWITCH
Your Susan fought bravely, but now she is as silent as the P in PTOLEMY.
Join the head girls' guild or DIE, Esther!
Get up, get up!
Let my bones knit first, Daisy.
Let my coccyx unbruise.
You horrible girls have *asked for it!*
Lollipop's staging a sit-in in protest!
FLOP
She's almost too adorable to *utterly destroy...*
ALMOST.

FACE THE AWESOME POWER OF YOGIC FLYING
What.
The awesome *untested* power of yogic flying
She's coming back around for a kamikaze strike!
She's crazy! Take cover!
Hey Daisy, I developed yogic flying for peaceful purposes.
Come down right now.
But but but but GEORGE HARRISON...
Yeah we're totally fight-ing them right now.
Yeah yeah. The little one's coming right at me.
Yeah I know, but I told her-
BLUNK

You have chosen your fate, Esther de Groot!
What do you want with me?
I like violent music, bleak books and subtitled films.
I DESPISE you!
I may as well come from *another planet* from you!
Head girls are a special breed!
Naturally selected over 7 years along strict Darwinian lines!
DESTINED TO RULE!
HOVER
HOVER
CRULLER DERBY
ED! QUICK! We've got about twenty seconds before they come out of exposition mode!
When a girl is born under a hunter's moon...
SPLÖG
WUNG
CRULLER DERBY
PLOP
PLOP

TUG
PSYCH
PSYCH
PSYCH
PSYCH
PSYCH
PSYCH
DUST
DUST
ESTHER DE GROOT
MARQUESS OF
QUEENSBERRY RULES
28 FIGHTS
WON 27
DRAWN 1
LOST 0

Ha ha ha, she boxes! The little goth boxes!
I've not finished my drink.
TAP
Take her down, Anna.
And look good doing it.
NYA!
NYA!
HA-CHA!
BLOCKBLOCKBLOCK
Anna, you've popped out!
DODGE
VOOP
No I haven't-
BOPP
DON'T UNDERESTIMATE THE POWER OF A PUNCH FROM A FOXY BOXER
BAT BAT
BAT

Your head girls' guild is defeated, Nita!
I suggest that you take your friends to HOSPITAL.
OR, how about I knock some colour back into your consumptive complexion?
I'm naturally PALE AND INTERESTING!
NOT
CRICKET
You're no match for NO STYLE!
How can THAT be "no style?
"No style" is *all styles* of fighting at once!
And you're *cupping* something that *doesn't belong to you!*
SWAT SWAT

I have no idea how you became head girl of your school.
But you'll be an example to future head girls of what happens when you go...
GURK
DRAG
...OFF MESSAGE
FSSSSSSS
FLIC
FLIC
What's that noise?
What's that *smell*?
SNIF
SNIF
FSSSSSSSS
AAAAAAAAA
Susan, you set fire to her hair extensions!
That's *brutal*.
FLICK
What do we do now?
Some might say setting fire to a crazy dame is going too far.
I say there's no such thing as too far. Only "just far enough".
Everything else I like to imagine as country they haven't made maps for yet.

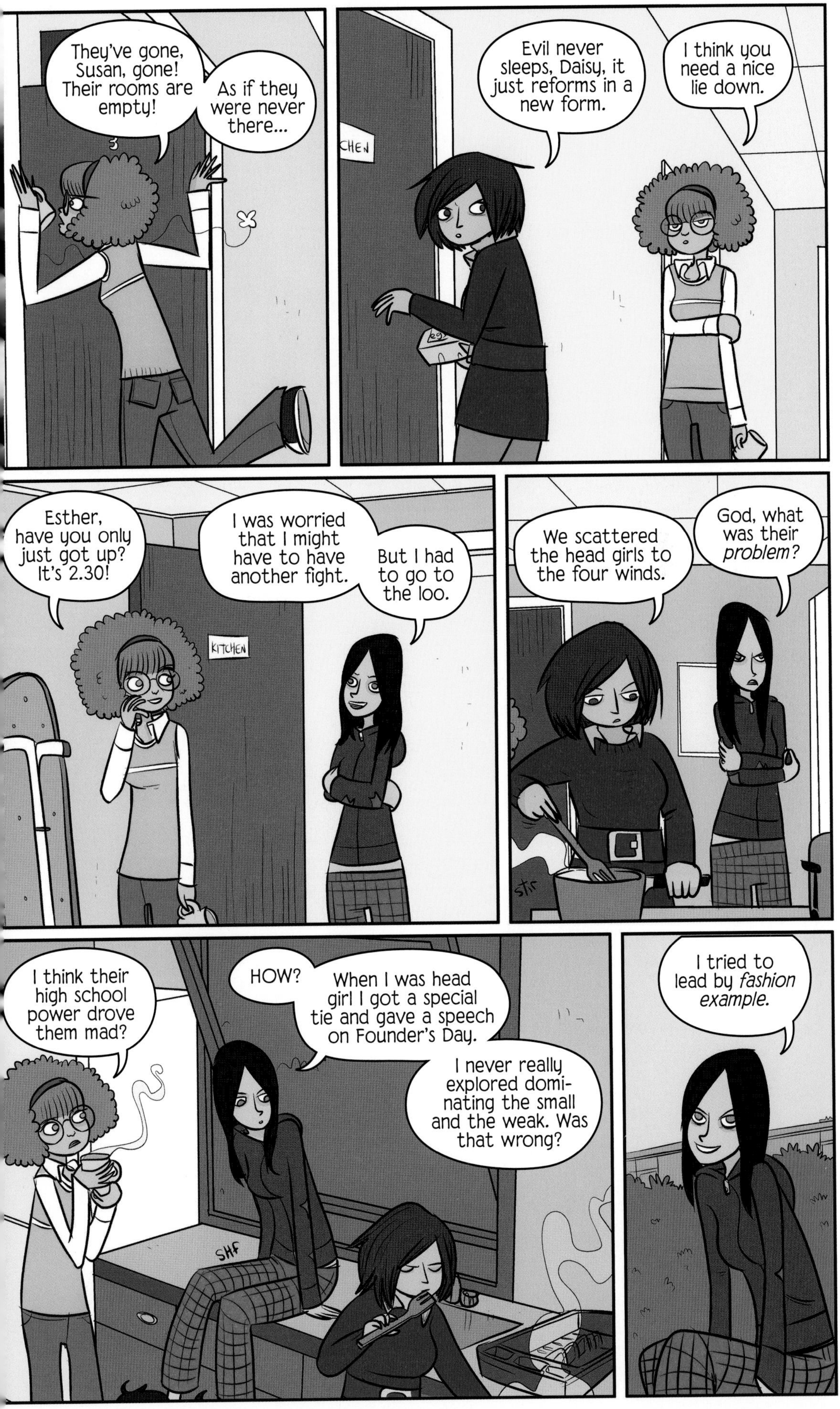
They've gone, Susan, gone! Their rooms are empty!
As if they were never there...
CHEN
Evil never sleeps, Daisy, it just reforms in a new form.
I think you need a nice lie down.
Esther, have you only just got up? It's 2.30!
KITCHEN
I was worried that I might have to have another fight.
But I had to go to the loo.
We scattered the head girls to the four winds.
God, what was their *problem?*
stir
I think their high school power drove them mad?
HOW?
When I was head girl I got a special tie and gave a speech on Founder's Day.
I never really explored dominating the small and the weak. Was that wrong?
SHF
I tried to lead by *fashion example.*

Eustace! My lovely boy! Mwa mwa mwa
You're being very generous with your kisses.
I missed you so much.
Me too. You look great. I like your new coat.
Good. Because I'm not wearing anything under it.
Whoa.
Except my CLOTHES.
GULP
So tell me about your first week!
Oh man, crazy! A lad on our floor drank so much that he had to go to hospital.
What about you?
Oh not much. A few run ins, you know.
Hi Ed Gemmell!
You need to get into my room very QUICKLY, Boyce.
I think I might be having a sexy episode

CHAPTER TWO

Taking in ironing is a genius money-making scheme, Susan.
You can look at your fellow freshers two ways, Daisy.
Our nation's future...
...or a lot of idiots whose mummies aren't clearing up after them any more.

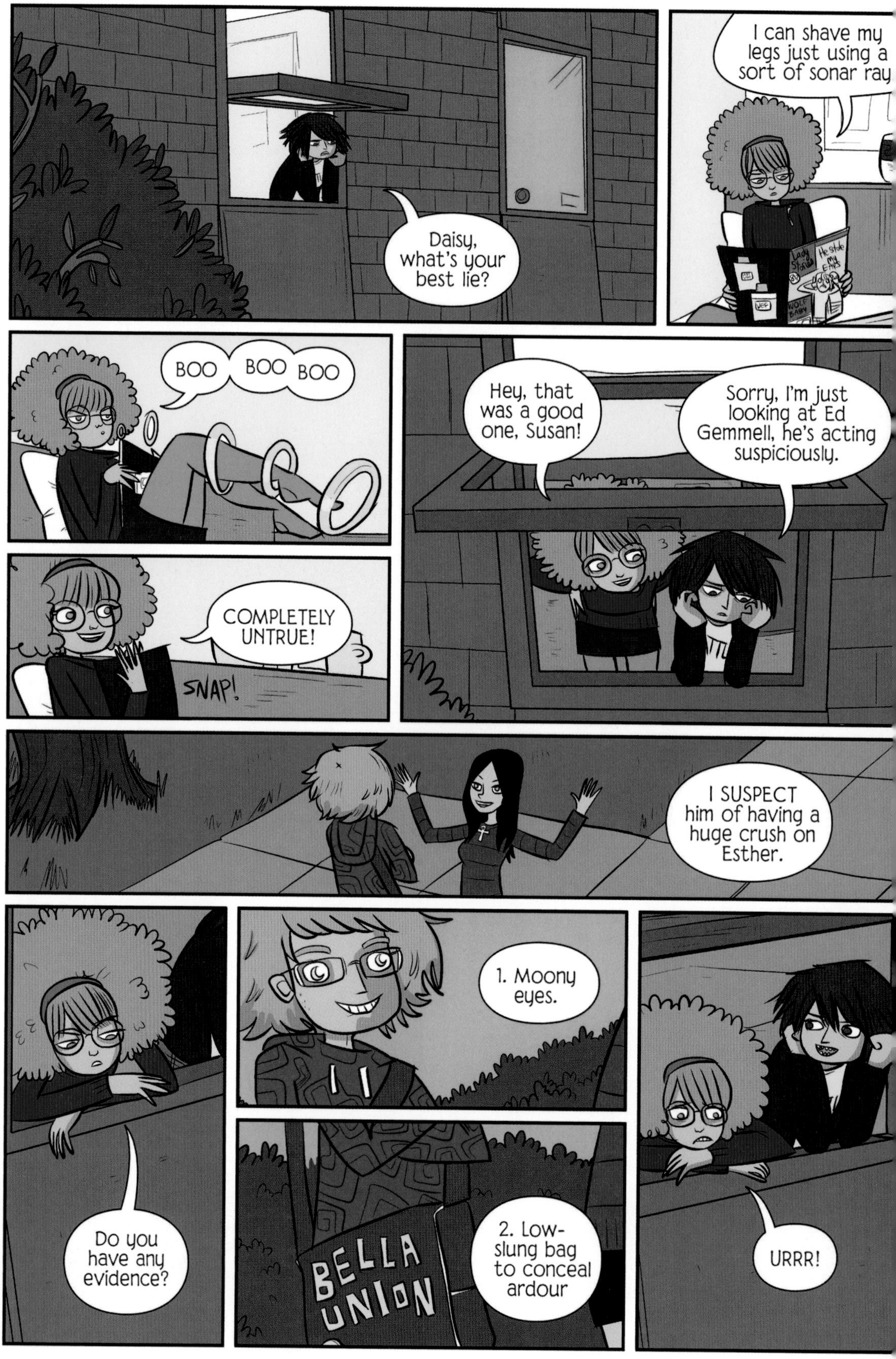
Daisy, what's your best lie?
I can shave my legs just using a sort of sonar ray
BOO BOO BOO
COMPLETELY UNTRUE!
SNAP!
Hey, that was a good one, Susan!
Sorry, I'm just looking at Ed Gemmell, he's acting suspiciously.
I SUSPECT him of having a huge crush on Esther.
Do you have any evidence?
1. Moony eyes.
2. Low-slung bag to conceal ardour
BELLA UNION
URRR!

Ed's a nice boy. Too nice.
Esther has a boyfriend. She'll break his heart.
PRIMP
Don't you *like* Esther?
Legs like rails, six feet tall, acerbic...
...what's not to like?
We need to break the spell she has on him.
CLICK
It's for the best.
The best way would be to engineer an EVENT.
Dress up as ghosts?
I thought, make it so he walks in on Esther and her boy...
...AT IT LIKE SHARP KNIVES.
Your mind is a cesspool, Susan!
GLOOP
She'll break his heart...
I-
...*you'll atomise his insides!*

...she's got a boy-friend, but he's not amazing or anything... he's just... normal.
And he's hours away, right? *Hours.*
McDonald
But you've made a mistake, mate, you've gone "straight to friend."
I reckon she likes me, you can sort of tell.
Yeah, sure, she likes you.
DRUM DRUM
But when you're alone she doesn't feel like she's...
...TRAPPED WITH A WOLF.
Er, no.
It's weird to think that yesterday we didn't even *know* each other!

That's her, that's Esther.
Hello Ed, whatcha doin'?
Nothing much. This is, er, Steve.
I found roller-blades at the charity shop!
Yeah? Yeah! Think of what you'll save on buses!
Yeah man. Well, see you later.
So what do you think? Is there some-thing there?
She's all sweet and touchy isn't she?
I don't know!
I don't know!
I don't know!
SCRUFF
I don't know!

Haha these are great!
Give it to me, I want to draw too.
There's some-thing about Ed, isn't there?
Yes! I think so, Susan.
STUB
Something that says he and his virginity...
...will be keeping each other company for a while.
Cruel! CRUEL!
CLOUD CONTROL
WOOT
So how *are* you going to destroy his Esther dreams?
I can't do it. Let nature take its course.
PROBLEMS SOLVED
"Who breaks a butterfly on a wheel"?
THE BADDIES.

THUD THUD THUD
THUD CHANG
THUD CHANG
It's 3AM, what the GEOFFREY BOYCOTT?
PWINK
PAD PAD PAD
KNOCK
KNOCK
KNOCK
Could you turn it down, please? I've got a nine o'clock lecture.
Yeah yeah, sorry.
Ah, sweet relief. Just goes to show, if you ask nicely-
THUD
THUD
THUD
-you've earned the right to be disappointed.

Did you hear it last night? Did you hear it?
SH
CLICK
Susan, you look TERRIBLE.
Daisy, get some teaspoons for her eyes.
SWEAR
Blah! Keep your witch-craft away from me!
SWEAR
On the boy floor above us, they were rocking ALL NIGHT.
Didn't you *hear?*
I'm a very heavy sleeper.
Of course you are. I suppose you are too, Daisy.
Oh no. I sleep with earplugs AND ear defenders.
SQUEA
Did you go up and knock?
Yeah, twice. Second time, no answer.
COWARDS.
What if there's a fire alarm?
I'm also woken by very strong SMELLS.
SNIFF

Are you ready to go?
Yeah, just come in a minute.
Your room is a PALACE.
I feel very inadequate about my life.
Thanks man. It's all right I guess.
BÊTES
Oh my God, that's beautiful, Steve.
It's a Kawai Flying Wedge. Vintage.
Employed in trained hands, its effects are LETHAL.
If you know what I mean.
THE FRENCH
Not really.
Chicks dig it.
PWANG PWANG PWANG
Can I play it?
Ed, you absolutely can't.
PLING

Oh hi, good morning Ed Gemmell, HI.
All right Esther. Have you done the reading?
Bloody hell, Ed, just give the teacher your apple and get it over with.
Hi Steve!
What do you reckon the saddest robot is, Ed?
I think it'd just be a robot head on top of an electric pylon.
FIXED.
Staring into the middle distance forever.
Yeah yeah, can't even move.
It's so DELICIOUSLY BLEAK.
Race you up to the bad kid seats!
I can't *believe* she has a boyfriend.
Plenty more fish, mate.
Put her out of your mind.

...which I expect you to have read by next Wednesday.
Nice notes.
FARTS FARTS FARTS
MICHAEL VAUGHN
Photographic memory, innit?
SNAP
Where IS the "Meffin Building"? We're going to be late.
Dunno mate.
I've not got anything on until four. I'll see you two later.
Oh, I see it!
Ed, I left my pen in the lecture, I'll see you up there.
Okay!!
Hey, Esther, wait!
Thought you had a tutorial.
I realised I had a finite time on earth, and reconsidered.
JOG JOG

Ron Lewis

HAHAH hahahha!!
Ha ha! I told you, pretending to be foreign in shops is the game that never gets old.
Your Dutch accent is very good...
...if we stretch the definition of "good" quite a long way.
Tell me about yourself, Steve Shields.
Where are you from? Is there a Mrs Shields? Any children?
I'm from Essex. Still not married. On the shelf.
Oh yeah SURE, the SHELF.
There was someone, but...
...it's gonna take a while to... you know...
Oh Steve! I'm sorry!
You know, she and I...
Sorry, it's my boyfriend, just a sec.
bzzt
bzzt
Oh nothing. Just in town with a friend.
He's chatty. For DEAD MEAT, I mean.

Ed Gemmell was tall and skinny with hair that looked like it could sue its owner for neglect and the eyes of a novice vicar.
Of all the corridors he could've loitered in, he chose mine.
Esther's not in, Ed.
Oh. She said she would be. I have a book to lend her.
I could be very unkind and say "I'll give it to her," but I'm not that cruel.
Come and have some soup.
I know she's got a boyfriend, but-
Let me guess, you've never met anyone like her.
Permission to be frank?
S-sure...
If you ever want to dip your wick at university, don't chase pretty girls with boyfriends.
YOU PLUM.
That was franker than I expected.

Where were you at break-fast, Susan?
Asleep. The night band kept me up until 5.
I think I'm losing my mind.
Let's get Esther for dinner.
She'll cheer you up.
Good idea.
She has the calm-ing manner of someone who's never had to wait for service in a bar.
WELL THEN DON'T BOTHER COMING AT ALL, EUSTACE!
Whoa, trouble in paradise!
BOP BOP
LET'S GO FOR DINNER.
Are you all right?
FINE.
Daisy, I've only been a medical student for two weeks...
...but I doubt Miss de Groot's self-diagnosis.
Pipe down, you QUACK.

I think we should have a big night out tonight. A BIG night.
Yeah, why not? The mother of all blowouts.
This is a lovely idea.
MORE DRINK, SUSAN.
Is it my round already?
This was a TERRIBLE idea.
Susan, this is ROCK NIGHT at the SLAG PIT.
I don't feel good about this place.
We're meant to be cheering Esther up, and this is what she likes.
COME ON! TIME TO DANCE!
I don't think this song is DANCEABLE!
GRAB
BOUNDARIES! PERSONAL BOUNDARIES!

Susan, I'm not... having a nice time.
WILT
It's half past one, I think you've suffered enough.
Esther, Daisy's had enough ROCK, let's go.
I'll go home when I WANT TO
MUM
What happened?
Come on Daisy, if she wants to be an ARSE, she can do it on her own.
HOO HOO HOO
Daisy why are you CRYING?
I'm sad. Tonight made me SAD.
Would chips and gravy help?
Can I have a sausage?

Mate, they turned off the music.
I don't want to stop dancing.
Is there anywhere we can go, Steve?
Not on a Tuesday night. Let's get home.
SLAG PIT
HAIL
PLIP
PWINK

Hey, Ed!
All right Steve!
This is my band. We're just going for a drink, wanna come?
Ivan!
Ash!
Sure!
Go on, Steve, tell us then, tell us ALL OF IT.
A gentleman never reveals his secrets.
Let's just say she had... *wide ranging interests...*
...and the best body I've ever seen in concert.
HEH
Who was it? Have I seen her about?
Ed... Ed... let's just say I didn't do anyone *you* wouldn't do.
No hard feelings?
COURSE NOT

Ed Eddy Ed Ed GEMMELL.
Stand up straight, boy, this is a man's army.
HEE! *Ed!*
Oh... hi.
What happened? Are you all right?
Did you witness a CRIME?
I... uh... well...
My mate Steve just told me he slept with Esther.
WHAT? Who's "STEVE"?
I've seen him. He's... quite short and wears an unnecessary hat.
Oh Ed. Well, I'm sure it's not true. Esther's well in love.
This Steve's just winding you up.
He's jealous of your friendship with her.
And your height. And your unashamed hatlessness.

Hi, you two.
I was just texting you to say sorry for being a flagrant dip-stick last night.
Sorry.
We're here with bad news. A... "Steve Shields"...
...is trashing your good name all over town.
WHAT?
Now I thought, to punish his lies...
...Daisy and I could duff up the soft parts of his body.
Then you could mess up his pretty face.
I... I...
AYE AYE!
...I did it with Steve.
BONK
Oh... ESTHER.
I was angry... I made a bad decision...
You didn't make a bad decision... *right here...* did you?

I had that fight with Eustace...
...but I miss him SO MUCH
And Steve... reminds me of him... in a way.
I wasn't that drunk, I was just...
EXTREMELY INJUDICIOUS.
Were you CAREFUL?
...I may have knocked his guitar off the wall and broken it...
...while *trying something.*
In a *prophylactic* sense, yes, but...
SAINTS ALIVE!
He wasn't pleased.
Ed Gemmell told us the guitar had magic powers over women.
Well, maybe if someone else was playing it, Daisy.
He made quite a stink come off that thing.
MERCY KILLING.

DAG DAG DAG DAG D
DA
AAARGHH!
This NOISE
is INTOLERABLE
It's LOUDER than WAR, Susan.
We're going to go up there Daisy, and-
WE'RE NOT GOING TO BE BRITISH ABOUT IT.
Adrenaline rush!!!
Just ride it out.
Who ARE these people?
Don't they have homes to go to?
DAG DAG DAG DAG
Oh no. This is a-
PART
-GUERILLA GIG.
Those parochial RUBES.

Turn this grisly jam the FLIP down.
WHAT?
I would like to speak to Steve Shields...
PRIVATELY.

Do you want us to stay?
Thanks Susan, but this is between me and Steve.
I can't sleep now! I feel all CRAZY!
Let's have a night sandwich.
Or a NIGHT EGG!
Ed, why are you wandering around like a ghost?
I couldn't sit still. Too many weird thoughts.
Thought I'd go for a walk.
I hope Esther's all right. Maybe we shouldn't have left her with Steve.
She's making
A TERRIBLE MISTAKE
Don't look at me like that!
HE DIDN'T WAIT FOR THE CONTEXT!

GIG TONITE
SCREECH
What am I DOING?
They're both adults... I shouldn't BE here.
You like me best, don't you babe.
Don't you.
Show me.
GIG TONITE
GET YOUR DAMN HANDS OFF OF HER!
FLING
GIG TONITE
Mate, *what?*
I was... I was... thinking of a different *her.*

Ed, come away, you shouldn't...
Oh no, Ed's already there.
BROWNIE
EEP!
WHOA MARY
We're going, we're all going, Steve.
I'm so sorry...
What's going on?
Esther, we thought you... er.... and Ed thought you...
What's in the bag?
Steve's precious guitar.
He won't be playing it in future without *forensic assistance*.
Come on Daisy. I'm sure Mr Shields and his new friend are very much in love.
Say what you like about the lad, he's an *operator*.
I only left 15 minutes ago.
She hadn't even had time to take her glasses off.
Can you have this conversation somewhere else?

No night band for three nights! What happened? Did they break up?
Well, I went to see the block representative to see if he could help.
Yeah mang, YEAH, night music. Cool.
I THINK HE'D BEEN SMOKING A DRUG PIPE.
CORN, FLAKED
He gave me a form to fill in...
The spineless worm.
So I scanned the top bit...
...used it to make a strongly worded official letter...
CATTERICK HALL
Dear resident,
Following a series of complaints, I must write to inform you that in the eventuality of further reports of loud music from other residents your position in hall will be under review.
OF OPERATIONS
6
...and posted it under Steve's door.
SLIP
I can't tell if that's passive, passive aggressive, or aggressive.
I just tried to imagine what Nelson Mandela would do!

Esther's still on the phone to her boy.
What do you think will happen?
If he's got any sense, he'll dump her.
SUSAN! Love must prevail!
She's someone who loves drama.
And she can get away with it.
Would you want to get sucked into a vortex of *drama*?
I don't want to get sucked into a vortex of anything!
What about poor Ed Gemmell?
We should help *him* find love.
That's so DARK, Susan. I think your life is like a garden.
You have to look after it.
You can't help most people. Life is a prison we build for ourselves.

I'm glad we're friends, Daisy.
Oh Susan, you're drunk.

CHAPTER THREE

You have to stretch first, Susan!
The sooner I start running, the sooner I can stop.
A few days of this and you'll be thanking me!
BROWNIE
Thanking you from *beyond the grave.*
We need to find a hobby, Daisy. Meet new people.
WHY?
Two's lesbians, three's a coven, and we don't even qualify as a coven any more.
I know. I miss Esther.
We weren't to know she'd break up with her boyfriend and lock herself away.
I feel like... we failed her.
You pushed Kraft cheese slices under her door to keep her alive.
I don't think you could have done any more.

Look at all these societies. One of them must be for us.
Yes. societies. I know about them.
I joined tabletop gaming society in freshers' week.
Yeah?
It was all tiny goblins and monsters, Susan.
I think they might have been SATANISTS.
SATAN is everywhere.
Indie society! Indie music, that seems safe.
They've got a meeting tomorrow evening.
Daisy, I thought you were a Buddhist.
Yes. But I spent a lot of time before Buddhism worrying about Satan.
I see... I see.
It's like a pop group you enjoyed as a child.
You know they're terrible now, but you still enjoy the songs.
Don't make light of SATAN!

Susan, I'm worried, I don't know anything about indie music.
I only like Enya.
Enya's the most indie recording artist of ALL TIME.
She's never played live. She lives on an island. She can probably FLY.
But this place will be full of "lads" with "opinions."
Don't tell them about Enya.
STOP
If anyone asks, tell them you've mostly been listening to the Disintegration Loops.
No one will challenge you on that.
Oh... okay... *I guess.*
Right. Are you ready to make new friends?
YES!
Mary and Joseph, look at this lot.
Thank ENYA there's not a war on.

Susan, we can't go home. Give it half an hour!
These... these... *are not my people.*
...I guess it's Radiohead #1 for me, then Postal Service #2.
Postal Service #1... then I reckon Radiohead second.
ALL OF MY BLOOD... IS BOILING
Come on, there must be someone here who looks like they'd be fun to be friends with.
Ah fink the Pipettes should be the new national anfem!
EH mate I'm just vibin' off it all.
If it's not real ale, I'm just not interested.
WOFF!
I love your glasses.
It's almost as if liking the same music...
...doesn't actually make you anything like anyone here.
I'm Erin.
Are you... a *mirage?*
LADIES
I want to go! Someone asked me to make them a "mix-tape!"

Hi, I'm Thom, acting president!
It's lovely to see so many of you here for Indie Soc.
Remember, we're looking for a new president and treasurer, so put your name down if you want to run.
"Acting president?"
Oh yeah! The previous administration was IMPEACHED!
It was a SCANDULE.
They spazzed all our subs on a big bag of drugs...
...then claimed they spent the money on "fixing the roof."
I AM AGHAST.
Thom rushed into the power vacuum like an *entitled gas.*
He's a big throbbing
RIGHT GUYS!
As an icebreaker, we're going to...
...name as many indie bands as possible.
PENS
This genius is wasted on the Indie Society.
He should be running the United Nations.

Vertical Helen.
Taupe Surprise.
Warned Off Milk.
WAXY?
The Congleton Bastards.
Hemp Problem.
The New Congleton Bastards.
The Congleton Bastards USA.
Okay guys! Stop naming bands now!
Besides myself, we've got a couple of names down for president.
Oliver Walton...
...and Felicity Baines-White.
A MILQUE-TOAST and PRINCESS EUGENIE
We're in for 12 months of Thom.
Okay, elections are next Wednes-day night, so-
I WISH TO RUN.
Okay! And you are?
SUSAN PTOLEMY...
...and I repre-sent a POWERFUL HYBRID OF HOPE AND CHANGE!

Is this it?
This is it.
This place is grim. It's like a jail.
I reckon you could well go mad in 'ere.
4J12. You knock.
No, you knock.
12
DO NOT DISTURB
KNÖCK KNÖCK
LISTLESS SCROLL
Esther de Groot?
Yes?
A message... from THE ROOK.
Oh-kay...
HISSSSSSSSSSSSSSSSSSSSSSSS
Attend
THE ENGINE, DIVISION ST
10PM-
Whoa!
Intriguing *and* annoying!

Wow! Your house is *big!*
How many people live here, Erin?
12. I don't know how they decide who lives with who.
It's like social engineering. "Meet your new friends."
METERS
What's that *smell?*
SNUFF
The kitchen. Let's not go in there.
Just let me take out my contacts. They're driving me mad.
Why do you wear them? Glasses are cool.
My sister looks like a glasses model in specs.
I look like someone cosplaying as my sister.
BADLY.
JAZZ
Right, who wants to be bad? I've got a whole area set up just for that.
I think for Daisy's sake, we should stick to... medium bad.
I'm on antibiotics!

Ha ha, Thom's face!
You TREATED that guy, Susan. You're going to take him to school next week.
Yes, yes
HMMM
Okay, good-night, thanks for saving me from IDIOTS.
Come round any time! You got my DIGITS.
Erin is FUN! I had FUN!
I don't know if Indie Soc is for me.
Pubs and drinking aren't really my sort of thing.
What did you do for fun back home?
Granny and I would do jigsaws sometimes.
Whoa, dial it down Caligula, once I hear these things I can't *unhear* them.
I miss Granny. A lot.
What was it like being home-schooled, Daisy?
I'VE NEVER KISSED A BOY AND I DON'T THINK I KNOW HOW TO DO IT RIGHT.
Limited curriculum. I see.

ATTEND! Attend what?
Who is "The Rook"?
Eustace, I'm so sorry for what I did. But I can't sit in here forever.
PLATH
ty Circular 60
DIVISI STREE
THE ENGINE
THE ENGINE
THE ENGINE

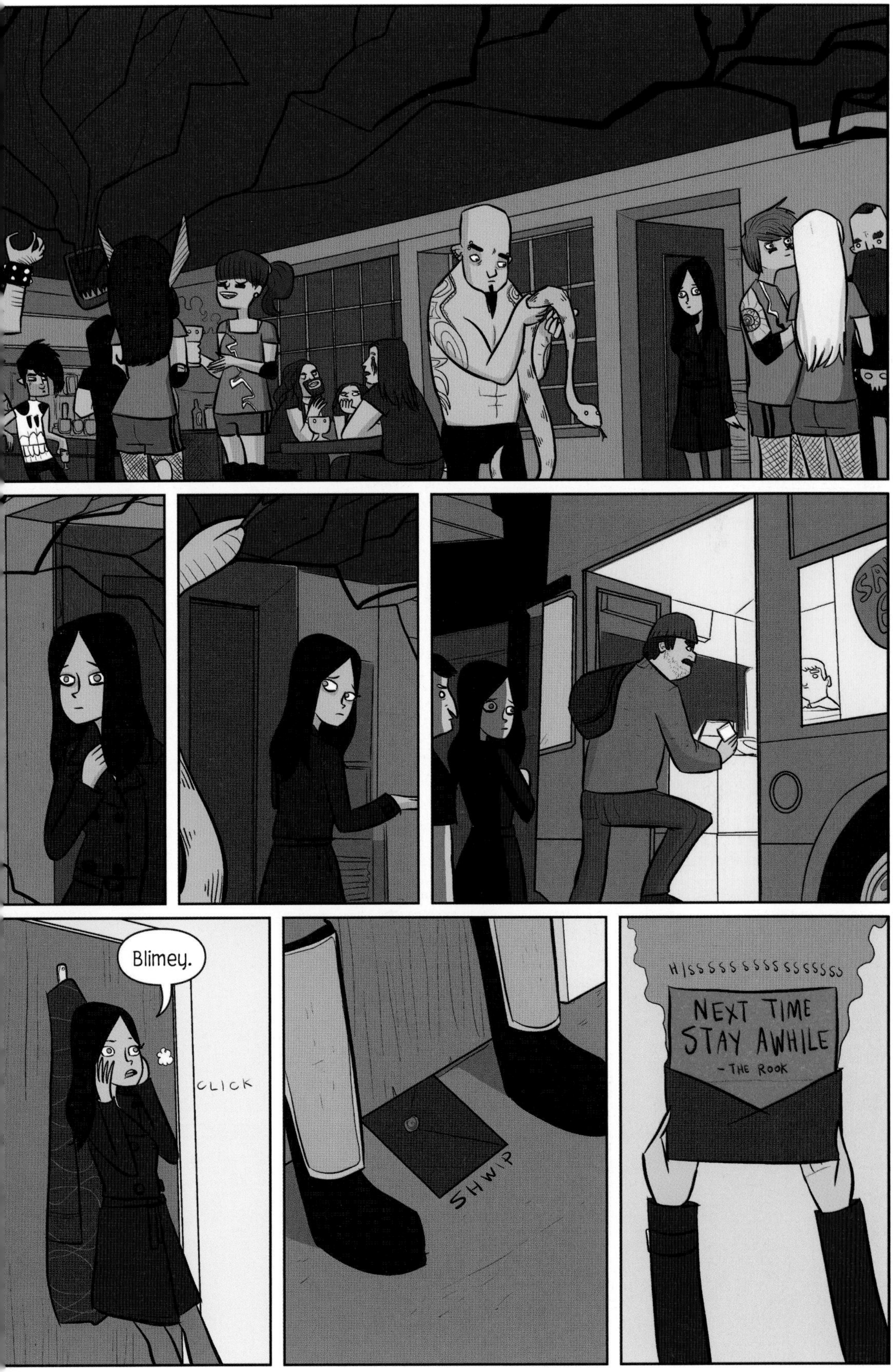
Blimey.
CLICK
SHWIP
HISSSSSSSSSSSSSSSSS
NEXT TIME STAY AWHILE
- THE ROOK

So you got there and it was just *Rock Society?*
Rock Society is a load of boofy lads in underwashed jeans and four girls.
This was like the military wing of Rock Soc.
A guy with a tattoo gun.
ZZZZZZZZT
Nasty drinks.
Jukebox playing music that sounded like it was having its guts ripped out.
It was... exciting.
It sounds... appallingly nightmarish.
Could they have been "cyber-punks?"
I want to go again.
I think we should *all* go!
There were ladies, Ed. Salty looking ladies.
They looked *easy to get on with.*
And you told me you LOVE metal!
I did... didn't I? Er of course I do.
Sure we can go.
Oh yeah and there was a SNAKE!
Of course there was.

We can do better, we must do better...
...we WILL do better!
I believe the independent spirit is something... blah-blah STUPID BLAH
TAP TAP TAP
I'm done working, do you want to watch a film?
Can't. Got to write my presidential speech.
It's currently presi-DON'T-shul.
YOU'VE GOT MAIL
SIGH
NEW CONTACT
Erin
Esther
Granny
Susan
What do you say to someone the first time you call them?
JAZZ
Daisy?
The more I look at my ceiling, the more I think it might be a treasure map.
Wow! I think things like that all the time.
You'd better come over. Bring a shovel and a compass.
I mean, if you got 'em.

Thank you very much for the meal, Erin.
FIRE BLANKET
Why thank *you*, Daisy. I opened the jar of pasta sauce myself.
SOY
Would you like a yogurt?
I only have the kind with a cartoon character on the pot and no health benefits.
Sure!
WHOOO ARGH
RUGBY SONG, RUGBY SONG, WE'RE SINGING A RUGBY SONG!
PUBLIC SCHOOL, PUBLIC SCHOOL!
BOF
Why is the kitchen full of GIANTS?
Let's eat this yogurt on the street.
For some reason, housing services decided I should live with the rugby team.
In fairness, some of them are the *women's* rugby team.
You must feel very... safe?
Yes, safe from a world where plugs remain unclogged with sick.

Isn't that Thom from Indie Society?
Yeah, with his pride and joy.
Hey THOM, what's going OM?
Heh, just giving Vetiver a polish.
"Vetiver"?
My 1990 Fiat Panda. Once owned by David Gedge of the Wedding Present.
PUT
T-CUT
Literally the most indie car EVER.
Fully restored. My parents got her for my 18th birthday.
POLISH
Great for getting to gigs. We don't get the good bands here very often.
Well, good-night Thom. Remember, *hands on top of the duvet.*
It's not the fact that he's got a car that annoys me...
...it's the fact that he asked for the most pathetic car in human history...
...and *pretends it's a woman.*

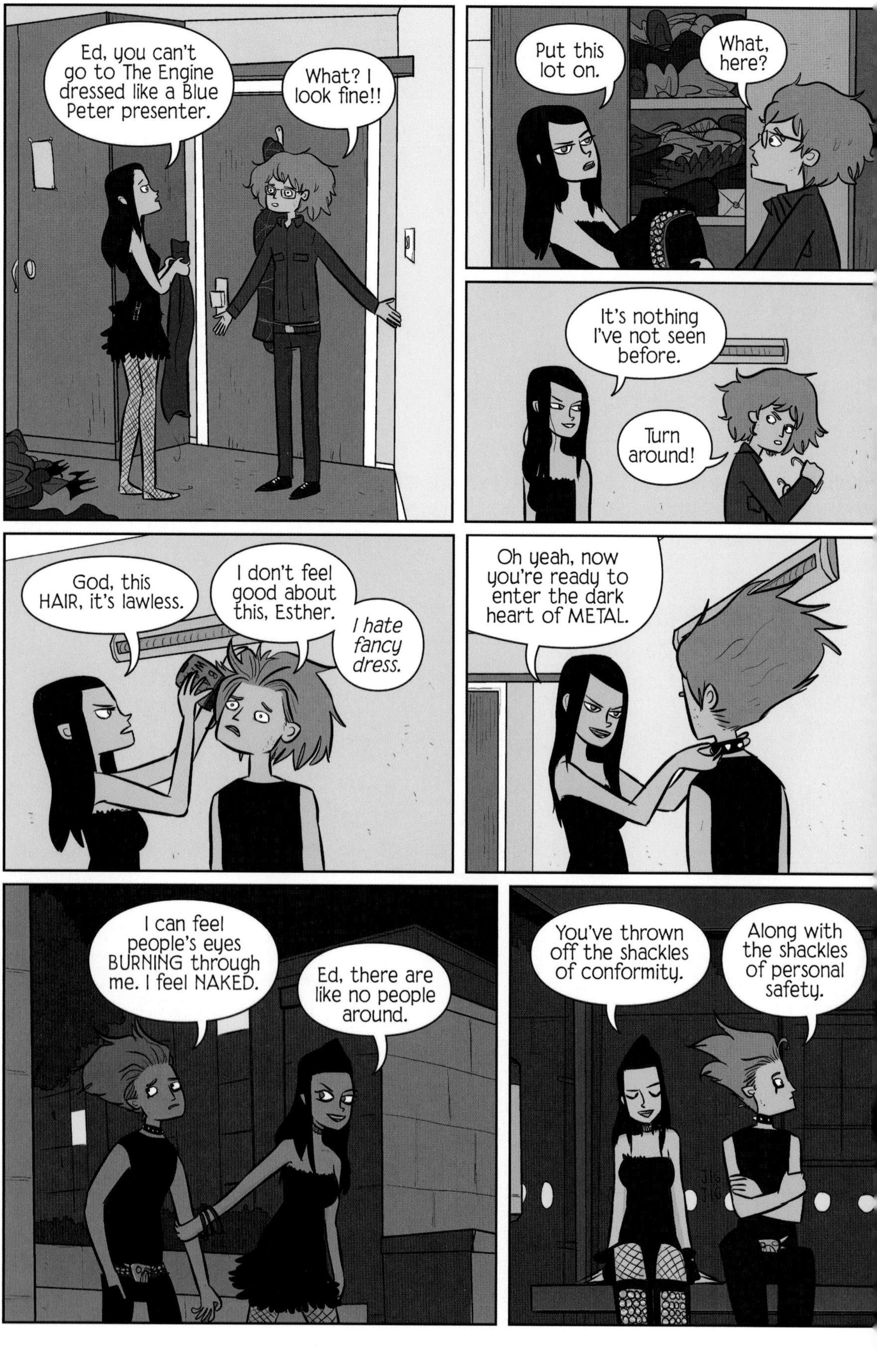
Ed, you can't go to The Engine dressed like a Blue Peter presenter.
What? I look fine!!
Put this lot on.
What, here?
It's nothing I've not seen before.
Turn around!
God, this HAIR, it's lawless.
I don't feel good about this, Esther.
I hate fancy dress.
Oh yeah, now you're ready to enter the dark heart of METAL.
I can feel people's eyes BURNING through me. I feel NAKED.
Ed, there are like no people around.
You've thrown off the shackles of conformity.
Along with the shackles of personal safety.

Don't be nervous, Ed, it's great in there.
SECURITY
It's so LOUD!
I KNOW! It's AMAZING!
YOU GO TO THE BAR, I NEED THE TOILET.
THERE'S NOT A LOT OF ROOM IN THESE NIGHT-MARE TROUSERS OF YOURS.
HOP HOP
HOP HOP
GENTS TOILET?
EART
THANKS -oop
SHOVE
PUSH BA TO OPEN
Where's Ed?
I think your friend bumped into someone he knew.
Private party mate, ticket only. Go home.
But I was just in there!
Careful Ed.
He's probably deciding whether to crush your head like a watermelon or a scotch egg.

You're Esther de Groot, right? You're a BNOC!
What?
A big name on campus!
Everyone heard how you fought those rich girls.
I'm THE ROOK. Welcome to BLACK METAL SOCIETY.
TOUCH
A BNOC...
Black Metal Society?
Er, do you know where my friend went?
I think I saw him copping off with one of the Maltby MW Roller Girls.
DOOK
Ed Gemmell, you sly dawg!
Come on, there are some people I want you to meet.
Sneaking in the toilet window? *Really*?
GRAB
NOB
FUNJYS
This hurts me more than it hurts you.
Think of it this way, you're saving the price of a bus ticket.
BOOT

AUGGHH... three o'clock? In the *afternoon*?
Those drinks must've been strong.
But my head doesn't hurt too much.
Stomach feels all right...
Why does my back hurt? I must've scratched myself.
You can't have a hangover...
...in your *back*.
OH... NO...
DAISY!
BOM BOM
SUSAN!
10
KNOCK
9
KNOCK
KNOCK
STUDENT... REPRESENTATIVE!
What do I have tattooed on my back?
It could be anything!
ALL THE CORN
Or... *everything*.

...in Indie Soc, we work hard and play hard. Vote THOM!
CLAP
CLAP
CLAP
CLAP
CLAP
CLAP
CLAP
SWIM DEEP
Hello.
I'm Susan Ptolemy. To show why I should be your president, I made a *cape*.
HOLY
WOW
On one side, I've written the names...
...of every band who ever made a human feel good to be alive.
CAMPER VAN BEETHOVEN
FENNESZ THE !!! WRENS SHELLAC
THE dBs
SLEATER KINNEY
MOUNT EERIE
ERIC B. + RAKIM GBV MBV
McCLUSKEY MASTODON
TELEVISION
CARIBOU ZAPPA JANDEK
BEACH BOYS FIELD MUSIC MAX LITTLE FEAT
On the other side, I stuck a picture...
SWOOP
...of a wolf on a skate-board in sun-glasses...
....doing a crooked grind on THE MAN.
ATP
I NEVER SETTLE FOR SECOND BEST-
-AND NEITHER SHOULD YOU!
I'm having an orgasm and the orgasm is also having an orgasm.
URRR!

The votes have been counted... *twice*...
...and the new president of indie society is-
SUSAN PTOLEMY.
Oh PLOPS!
CONVERSE
I promise a better deal for everyone.
My door is always open.
Brightly coloured drinks are on ME!
DRAUGHT
GUINNESS £3
MAC + CHEESE
LASAGNE
BLUE CHEESE BUR
She won it with that CAPE, it's RIDICULOUS.
Thom, that's the lager talking, you need a real ale to mellow you out, woff.
SUSAN I CHALLENGE YOU!
DOUBLE OR QUITS!
For the presi-dency? But what would you offer me if you lose again?
ANY-THING.
How about... *really*? Your beloved CAR?
WHISPER
BRING IT ON... YOU SHOWBOAT-ING LADY CHARLATAN!
Come on Thom, have a sip... it's organic with citrusy high notes.

Ed, hey Ed Gemmell.
GLOBAL
CES
Ed?
STAB
AAH AHH! Don't creep up on someone like that!
You have the mark now.
Join us here for FINAL INITIATION.
St Matthew's church GRAVEYARD at midnight? Are you ruddy kidding me?
HISSSSSSSSSSSS
You're sitting on your own, eating terrible food, talking to nobody.
Of course you'll be there.

I challenge you to a DRINKING CONTEST.
You've had enough to drink, son.
Plus, you're a foot taller than me...
...and that beer belly's *the fuel tank for a sex machine* if I'm not mistaken.
POKE
Let's settle this like JEFF GOLDBLUM in THE FLY...
...with an ARM WRESTLE.
I won't arm wrestle a girl.
SWIM DEEP
OH? Think you'll lose? Look at that bicep.
SWIM DEEP
It looks like a strip of Wrigleys on top of a dog's bone.
I guess *hand-wringing* doesn't build much muscle.
CHALLENGE ACCEPTED.
BRUSH
I won't snap your arm, Brundlefly style.
At least, not on purpose.
WATNEY'S "The Flavour"

3-2-
1
DEEP
SWIM
SLAM
Keys and V5C certificate, please.
WINTERS
The funny thing is, I can't even drive, Thom.
I can!
Well, there you go Erin, I guess you have a car now.
What's going to be your first decree as Indie Soc president?
I RESIGN.
Susan Ptolemy seeks dominion over no man.
Oliver, you're president now.
OH, GLORY BE!
That feeling, Oli....
That's *women wanting you.*

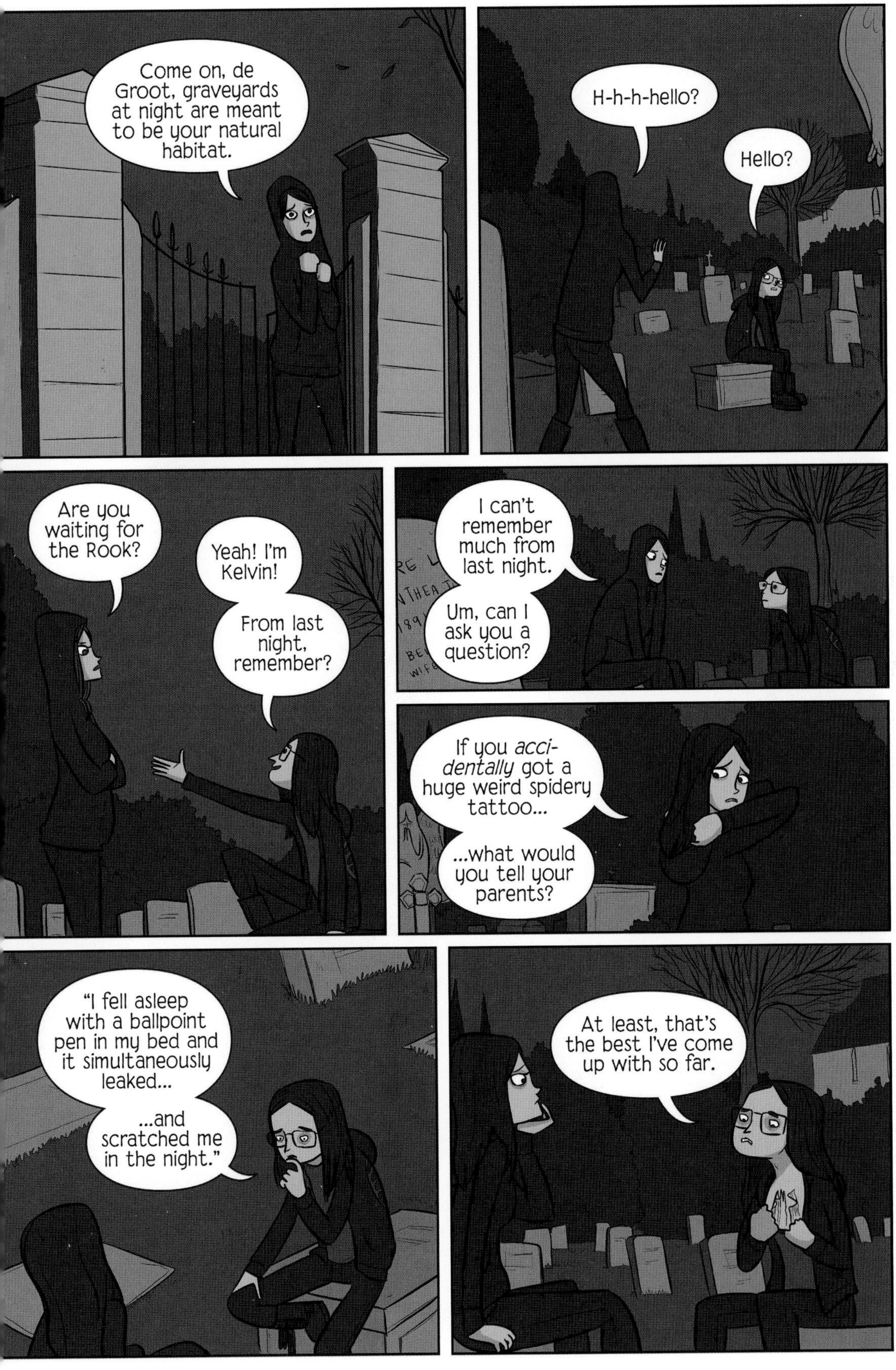
Come on, de Groot, graveyards at night are meant to be your natural habitat.
H-h-h-hello?
Hello?
Are you waiting for the Rook?
Yeah! I'm Kelvin!
From last night, remember?
I can't remember much from last night.
Um, can I ask you a question?
If you *accidentally* got a huge weird spidery tattoo...
...what would you tell your parents?
"I fell asleep with a ballpoint pen in my bed and it simultaneously leaked...
...and scratched me in the night."
At least, that's the best I've come up with so far.

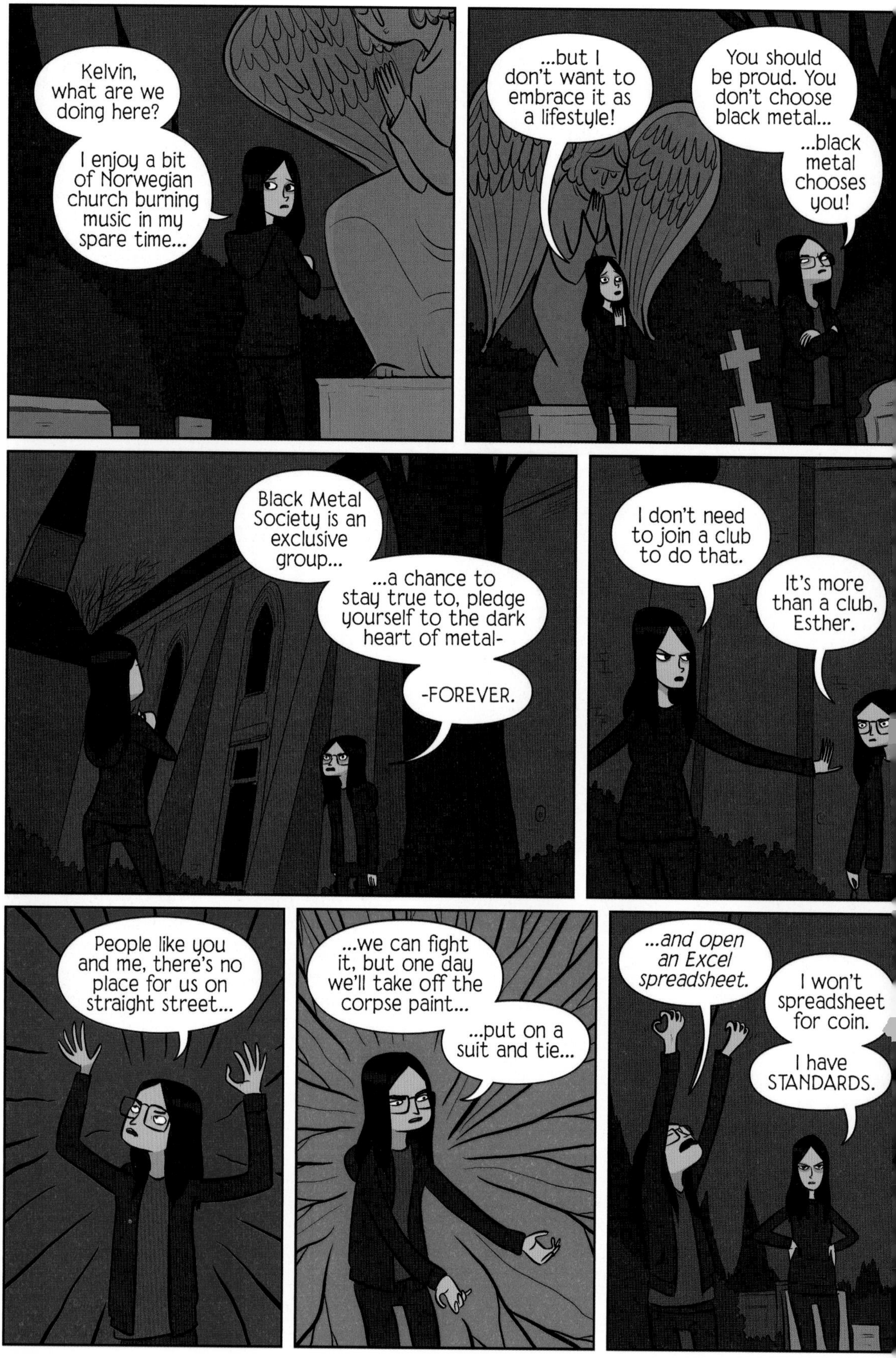
Kelvin, what are we doing here?
I enjoy a bit of Norwegian church burning music in my spare time...
...but I don't want to embrace it as a lifestyle!
You should be proud. You don't choose black metal...
...black metal chooses you!
Black Metal Society is an exclusive group...
...a chance to stay true to, pledge yourself to the dark heart of metal-
-FOREVER.
I don't need to join a club to do that.
It's more than a club, Esther.
People like you and me, there's no place for us on straight street...
...we can fight it, but one day we'll take off the corpse paint...
...put on a suit and tie...
...and open an Excel spreadsheet.
I won't spreadsheet for coin.
I have STANDARDS.

Do you have friends here? Do you feel like you belong?
I... I don't!
That light!
FALL ON ME, O BA'AL! GREAT DECEIVER!
I told you it was her!
Esther, what are you doing loitering in a graveyard?
You're old enough to drink in pubs now.
BOW
Oh, hello!
SSSS!
I just wanted... to make friends.
We're your friends, you big fanny.
Have you returned from your holiday up your own arse?
Um, yes. Do you have a car now?
Susan won it by destroying a man's way of life.
Of course she did.

They gave me this stupid tattoo and I don't know what it SAYS.
It's black metal writing. B-M-S. "Bowel Movement Society."
Very responsible. Fibre is important.
Are these your new friends?
Did they go to Tesco's to get you some WKD?
It's the Black Metal Society coming to initiate me.
We'd better go.
HERE LIES HOPE ETERNAL
Are you coming, Kelvin?
Er, no! I didn't get this tattoo for nothing.
Um, yeah, okay, so, nice meeting you!
RMMMMMMM
Watch the gatepost!
SCRAP
Oh, that'll buff right out.

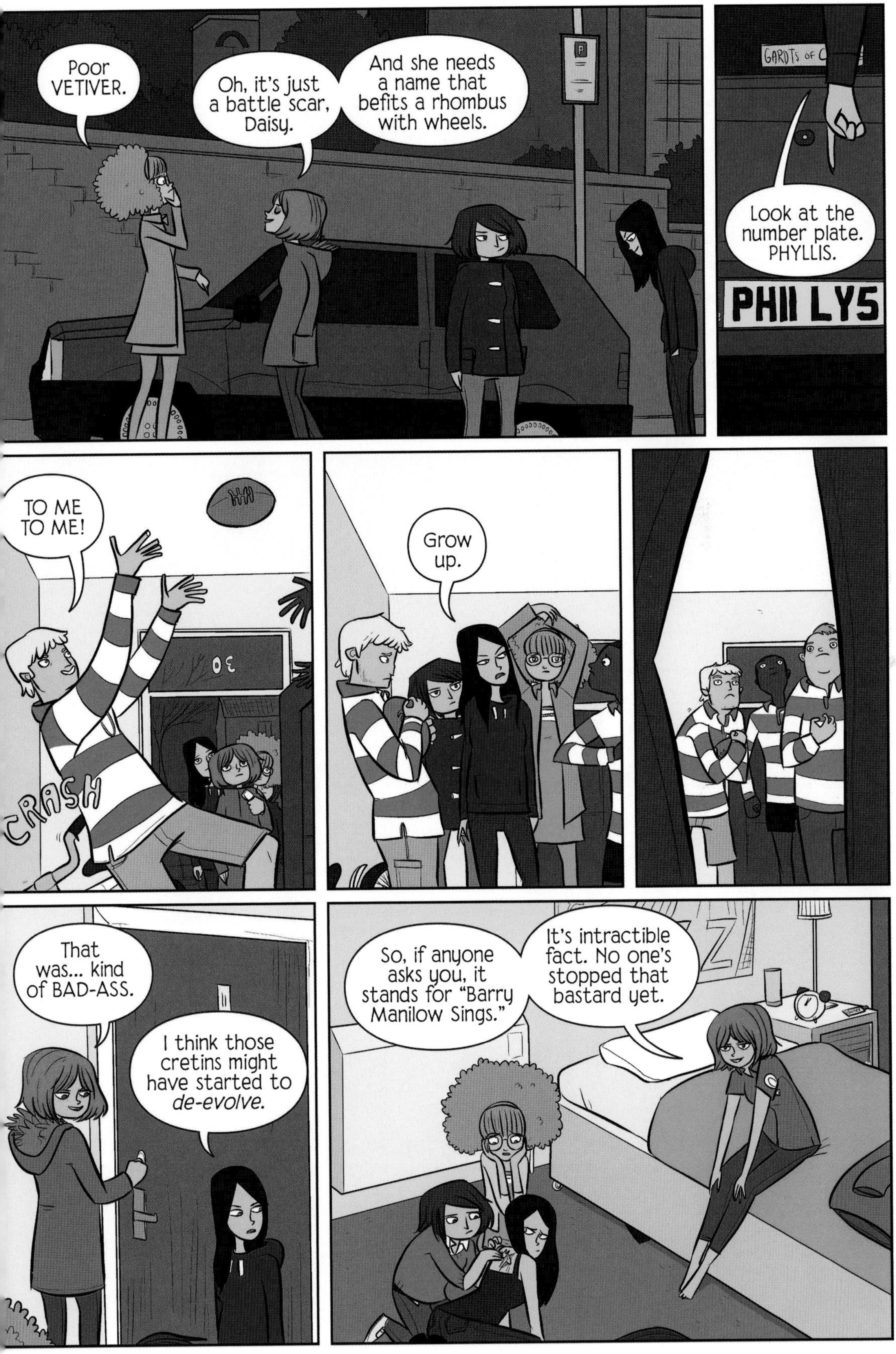
Poor VETIVER.
Oh, it's just a battle scar, Daisy.
And she needs a name that befits a rhombus with wheels.
Look at the number plate. PHYLLIS.
PHII LY5
TO ME TO ME!
CRASH
Grow up.
That was... kind of BAD-ASS.
I think those cretins might have started to *de-evolve.*
So, if anyone asks you, it stands for "Barry Manilow Sings."
It's intractible fact. No one's stopped that bastard yet.

With the solemn authority of both KING and QUEEN, I, the ROOK...
...induct you, Kelvin Bowbotham, into Black Metal Society.
To complete the circle...
...put your hand...
...in the box.
HISSSSSSSSS
SWING
QUIVER
AIIIIIIIEEE
What was old is new again, and at once ancient as time.
You wanted the cream of the crop, but you got the crumbs.
Never mind.
Until the sun turns black and dies...
...there will always be second chances.

ORIGINAL COVERS BY

JOHN ALLISON

GIANT
DAYS
JOHN ALLISON

GIANT DAYS
THE ORIGINAL SERIES
by JOHN ALLISON
2 OF 3

GIANT DAYS

JOHN ALLISON

2

John Allison

3

COLOR TEST FOR GIANT DAYS #2

EARLY CHARACTER DESIGNS (AND NAMES!)

DEVELOPMENT SKETCHES

DARKSOC

Open & shut cases
grr!
WINK
THUMBS UP

ALBUMS OF THE YEAR, SUSAN?
Rubbish! where is the Rock?
Is there any Enya? She's got some good songs! ORINOCO FLOW!
You two are WELL BAD AT MUSIC.
Esther only likes ICY SOUNDSCAPES AND GUTTERAL DRONING...
Yeah, what of it?
michael Dell
And Daisy is a new-age MANIAC
POKE
Music should be soothing, like whale song, but with SYNTHESISERS

Kelly Voltran
Abigail Dennis
Ed Gemmill
EDD GEMMILL
Steve Shields
Aaugh Blerg
Blaugh

Esther de Groot
Susan Ptolemy
Daisy Minter
I had to go into REHAB for overusing twitter!
I'm EXTREMELY COMPULSIVE:

SUSAN
STINKERS

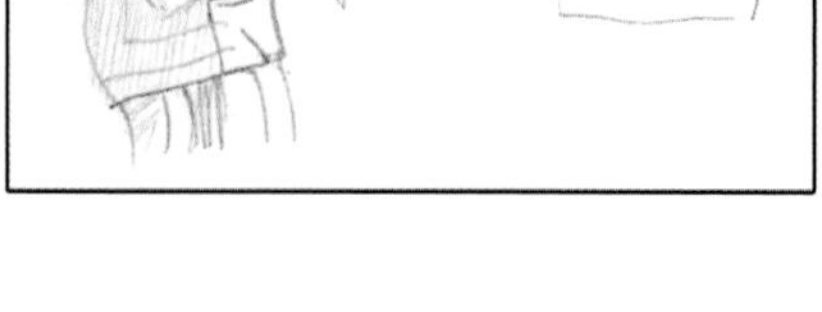
HA HA HA HA HA HA HA HA
MACK

Soothing
Don't get too wide
BITCHES
Susan, they're not worth your trouble
DAISY BOTTON
EVERYTHING IS IN ORDER
SUSAN PTOLEMY

THE TEAMS THAT MEET IN CAFFS
They're vacant
They're a bunch of vacants
SUSAN!
If you can't say anything nice, don't say anything